CURSES AND OTHER FAMILY SECRETS

R.R. BORN

With all your flaws and all your doubts-
You are special. You are unique.
You are enough.
Never doubt it.

WELCOME HOME

New Orleans is a magical place, to be sure, but visiting in February can also be the biggest pain in the ass. There will always be an endless supply of drunk tourists any time of day or night, mile-long traffic around the French Quarter, and someone flashing their titties. Not to mention the public sex. Up against a wall, down an alley, or on a counter in the bar restroom. None of those places provided the privacy some thought it did. Roz had seen her fair share of full moons. Even with all of that being said, this place still had the best food and the most amazing people in the world.

Clover, Rozlyn's mom, had moved the family to Houston after getting into a heated argument with Gran. Roz remembered it clearly because it happened the day she turned thirteen, at the last birthday party she ever had. In New Orleans or anywhere. That was twelve years ago.

Over the years, she wanted to visit so many times, but her mom had forbidden it. Truthfully, by the time she turned twenty, she could have visited. Clover cared little about what she did. Unless Roz mentioned Louisiana, and then all bets were off. Clover would become the most involved mother on the planet for the next week or until Roz acted like she no longer had any interest in going. No one in the family talked about it, but her mom might be legitimately certifiable.

It took every bit of willpower in Roz to keep her fingers from trembling as she moved the long gray strands away from her grandmother's face, then kissed her cheek. It was hard to see Rosa Marguerite Delacroix—or Mama Flora as everyone called her—a woman was once the epitome of strength and vitality, like this. Now, her face was thin, and her body looked like it would snap in a powerful gust of wind.

How long has she been sick?

Roz was well into her twenties—hell, she could see thirty waving its hand in the distance—nevertheless, no one told her anything.

Flora turned her head, opened her eyes, and gave a weak smile. Her seemingly frail hand slid from under the colorful patchwork quilt and Roz took it gently.

"Sweet Rose, I didn't think you'd make it," Flora whispered as she touched Roz's cheek.

Although her name was Rozlyn, Gran had always insisted on calling her Rose. Tears welled in her eyes, but didn't fall. If her grandmother passed away, no one would ever call her that again. This thought alone made Roz melt deeper into her grandmother's touch. She inhaled, and the fresh scent of Dove soap enveloped her, a fragrance which took her back to her childhood. Her grandmother always put the pieces too small to bathe with inside little cloth bags inside drawers in every room, scenting the entire house.

Roz's desire to come back to New Orleans hadn't been about the city or this old house, but about this woman. She had a way of making Roz feel loved with a simple caress of her fingertips. Also, Gran was the only person who could touch Roz without causing debilitating pain. The doctors had misdiagnosed her condition a few times. Tactile Allodynia is what they diagnosed with, but they weren't sure if that was what she really had.

Correct or not, her affliction had gotten to the point where she wore gloves all the time, so to not touch anyone by accident. Even the slightest brush against someone would make her topple over in agony. Anyone alive anyway.

"I've missed you so much. I just got busy, you know," Roz said.

A look passed between them. They both knew she hadn't been *that* busy.

Flora struggled to push herself up. "Help an old woman up, dear."

Roz grabbed her by the arm and helped her sit up, placing the pillow snug behind her back. "You're not old."

Flora harrumphed. "You tell my achy bones that. Now, explain why you haven't visited me."

Roz looked away. "You know how Mom is."

Flora *tsked* her. "Don't lie to your granny, girl." She tapped her temple.

Well, what she'd said about her mother was mostly the truth. Roz nodded and laughed. "That's right, your powers."

For years, people in the neighborhood said her grandmother knew about things before they happened. Roz believed it, as every woman in her family had some type of power, so strange things always happened to them. Well, everyone except her. She couldn't talk to animals or see the future. That wasn't so bad, she just wished she could touch one person. It would be nice to be special, like the rest of her family.

"All I'm going to say is your younger brother found his way here before joining the service."

Of course, it would have to be her *perfect, never do anything wrong,* brother. He was also the smart one, getting away from Clover at the first opportunity. It was the only way to preserve anyone's sanity.

Roz looked down at her fidgeting hands. "There's no excuse. Not a real one, anyway."

Gran touched her cheek. "I figured as much."

Lifting sorrow-filled eyes, Roz studied her grandmother. It was difficult to believe this woman was sick at all. "What is it, Gran? Why are you looking at me like that?"

Flora's smile widened as she lowered her hand. "You turned out to be such a beautiful young woman. What are you now? Twenty-three…twenty-four?"

"Twenty-five," Roz admitted, then heaved a heavy sign. "I'm practically an old maid."

"Not hardly, dear." Flora patted her hand. "Now, tell me. You have a young man?"

Her cheeks flamed. Roz leaned back and simply shook her head. How could she explain to her grandmother how being touched, or touching anyone else, caused unbearable pain?

No relationship could withstand that little quirk.

At some point, the guy—or girl, she wasn't picky at this point—would want to kiss her, hold her, hug her, make love to her…and she simply could not do it.

Fate had laid out the terms for her solitary existence years ago.

Flora nodded her head like she understood, then patted the bed. Roz took a seat next to her.

"I need for you to do me a favor."

"Anything, Gran, you know that," Roz said.

"Today is Mardi Gras."

She smiled. "I know that. I'm sure the whole of Louisiana knows it, too."

Gran patted her hand in a *bear with me* touch. "There's a band playing at the Thorny Rose I like."

Roz rolled her eyes. "Gran, that's in the Quarter," she whined.

Flora laughed and stroked Roz's arm, almost like she was soothing a wild animal. "I know exactly where it is. If I could go, I would."

If Gran would have pouted as one tear streamed down her face, the guilt trip would have been complete. With her eyes closed, Roz lowered her head, and said nothing. Of course, she'd do this for her grandmother and anything else, if the woman asked. Even drive to the French Quarter, go to a crowded bar during Mardi Gras, and listen to a band. Wow, she loved this woman.

"I must live vicariously. Hey, can you do that thing the kids do now... livestream it? If they give you any trouble about recording it, ask for the owner, Francois. I've known him for years. He's a bit of a man-whore, but an overall good egg," Flora said.

"Gran!" Roz exclaimed with mock indignation. "Language."

"What? He is."

They both giggled like tweens, but once that died down, Gran cleared her throat. "I appreciate you doing this for me. I really would like to hear them..."

There was something in her voice. Like if she'd finished that sentence, she would've said, *"One last time."*

Roz shook the morbid thought away, grinned, then spoke in a playful tone. "What-chu know about live-streaming?"

"Young lady, I'm old—not senile."

They laughed.

Gran patted her hands together like a little kid. "Oh, when you get there, go to the bar. They make this superb drink. Oh, what's it called? They gave it a silly name, but I can't remember it." She paused for a beat or two, then said, "It's a Dewberry Gumdrop martini." She smacked her lips as if she could taste it.

Roz eyed her suspiciously. "What's in it?"

"Nothing bad. If I can drink it, surely you can too." The older woman gave her a sly look, an almost dare. "And get a tequila shot chaser."

"What? No." Tequila was not her friend. The first and last time she'd tried it, clothes went missing, and she almost got arrested.

"Did you or did you not just say 'anything'?" She arched an eyebrow … waiting.

If Roz didn't know better, she'd say her grandmother was challenging her. Meeting her grandmother's challenges always led to nothing but trouble, and today was no exception. "Gran, you just don't understand. Me … tequila. We don't get along."

The old woman squinted, eyeing her with suspicion. "Something you want to tell me?"

Oh, God no.

Waving her hands in surrender, Roz relented. "Fine, fine. I'll go."

"Who knows? You might need that shot before the night is out." Gran winked and smiled.

Roz hopped off the bed and headed to the chair to get her purse and cardigan. "I better get going then."

The bedroom door opened, and Great Aunt Fauna leaned in, holding onto the door handle. "Is it time?"

Flora nodded towards the door.

Roz looked between her gran and her great aunt. "Gran?" She watched the door shut behind Fauna. "What's going on?"

She didn't have to be a soothsayer to sense something was about to happen. Only moments ago, they were laughing and having a good time, but now the vibe had dropped off. Now, it felt like her grandmother was sending her to this bar for a reason. Nerves fluttered in her tummy. It was the first time something like this had ever happened around her grandmother.

A sad smile turned up the corners of Gran's mouth. "Rose, before you go. I have a gift for you."

2

THE GIFT

A gift isn't a bad thing.

Any other day, this is what Roz would have thought, but Gran looked absolutely miserable. Gift-giving and receiving should come with a smile, maybe even a song. All of the sudden, the room felt drafty. Roz left her purse in the chair but put on the cardigan. Holding herself tight, she paced.

"Rose, come. Sit. It's nothing terrible."

"You say that, but the look on your face screams something different." Instead of sitting, Roz stood at the foot of the bed. "You aren't telling me something. What is it?"

They stared at each other.

"I can't believe your mother didn't tell you this years ago," Flora grumbled out loud. She sighed, then looked Roz straight in her eyes. "Rozlyn, our family—"

The door opened behind them. Roz turned slightly to see Aunt Fauna walk past her with a cat on her heels. Arness was not a house cat, but an ocelot and new to the Delacroix household. Her aunt had rescued exotic and domestic animals for as long as she could remember. She'd often said she preferred animals to people because they held better conversations.

Fauna held a small wooden box in both her hands. She gave it to Flora as she asked, "Do you want me to stay?"

"Please."

Fauna nodded, then took a seat in one of the wingback chairs near the window. Roz moved from the end of the bed to the side. She'd seen this box once before. As a kid, she and her best friend Aurora had been playing hide-and-seek in the house, where they'd found the box hidden in the back of a closet.

"May I?" Roz's fingers longed to touch it.

Flora turned the box towards her. "We live in a different world than what you see around you."

Roz's fingers grazed over the box, then halted. "How?"

Gran exhaled. "It's a long story. Just know that you *are* special, too."

Roz traced a finger along the grooves of the crescent moons carved into the surface of the old wood. "Like Aunt Fauna with animals or Mom's insane strength?" *Insane being the operative word.*

"Not quite, I could tell you, but it wouldn't make sense. Honestly, you probably wouldn't believe me, anyway. Soon enough, you'll learn all about it."

Touching the box somehow felt reverent. "You know I'm not like them, or you, for that matter."

"I know you better than you know yourself."

That's probably true.

Roz nodded and turned the box back around. "This is so beautiful."

"It's been in our family for generations."

Gran unhooked the brass clasp to open the box, and a faint scent of cedar filled the room. Odd that an antique box could still smell like a fresh cut tree. Inside, on a bed of black, shiny satin, a ruby ring glinted in the light, along with a few gemstones and a skull brooch with amethyst eyes.

When she was younger, Gran had let her try the ring on a few times, but it was always too big. The ruby and the swirls around the skulls were still as mesmerizing to her now as they had been when she was a child. There was something about the piece which just drew her in and made her want to touch it.

Her grandmother held it out to her.

She shook her head. "Oh, no Gran. I can't." Whipping her hand behind her, as she took a step back.

Flora extended the ring out farther. "Please."

Roz didn't know why this moment felt like something important. This wasn't like playing dress-up years ago. She didn't want to think about it too much, but an energy pulsed from the ring. Dare she even think it?

Magic.

It called to her, and her feet moved of their own accord. With her right hand extended, one step, then two, she eased forward.

Gran slid the ring onto Roz's index finger. "All that I do now … remember." Gone was the soothing, soft voice, which held laughter and joy.

Each word her grandmother spoke held a power. A small ripple of energy moved all over her body and seized her, paralyzing her to that spot.

Their gazes met, and Roz knew it, felt it. Her entire life she knew her family was weird but had thought nothing of it. Now, she wondered, *Are we witches?* Energy emanated from the ring in a faint, red wave. It moved from the ring towards her in an undulated motion.

Is this how magic looks? Moving all around like rivers.

Roz couldn't turn away from it. "Gran, can you see that?"

"Yes, child. I do, and if you can see it, then you are the right person for the job."

Job? What job? Roz wanted to ask, but Gran seemed to be adamant about the things in this box. Her questions could wait.

Gran reached into the wooden box again and pulled out the skull brooch. The amethyst eyes glistened in the lamplight as she pinned it on Roz, pricking her skin under the shirt.

Roz yipped from the sharp sting.

"Sorry," she said as she cupped her granddaughter's cheeks.

A voice yelled from behind them. "No! Stop, Momma!"

Roz didn't need to look back to know who was there. She attempted to turn her head, anyway, but Gran's grip was unyielding. Until this moment, her grandmother didn't seem to have much strength. Looks could be deceiving.

A low feline hiss and growl filled the small bedroom.

"Fauna, call off your damned hellcat," Clover demanded.

A chair scraped along the hardwood floor. Although Roz couldn't turn her head, she figured Aunt Fauna must have moved from her seat to stop her mother from interrupting. The growl grew louder.

"I'm sorry. Arness does what she wants and right now she wants you to stay put."

"Dammit, Mother. Don't do this," Clover pleaded.

Gran acknowledged nothing being directed towards her, instead kissing one of Roz's cheeks. "I give thee knowledge." She leaned in, softly kissing her forehead. "I give thee sight, beyond sight. To know right from wrong in a person's heart."

"Don't!"

Clover sounded like she was about to cry. Which was a little disturbing, because in Roz's life, she'd never seen her mother cry once or show any other type of emotion. This day was a day of revelations.

Gran kissed the other cheek. "I give thee compassion." She stared into Roz's eyes. "I give thee my eternal love." Then, she whispered, "I'm sorry."

Roz opened her mouth to ask why, but Gran moved too fast when she pressed her lips to Roz's. Warmth stemmed from where their mouths were connected. Roz winced when the sensation went from heat to pain. She tried to yank back but couldn't. It felt as if she were being singed from the inside out, from her hair follicles to her toenails.

Tears ran down her Gran's face. Roz didn't seem to be alone in her agony. She just wanted this torture to stop. Who knew pain could be this overwhelming? Closing her eyes, thinking it would help, Roz felt a sharp pain which stabbed, poked and prodded until they snapped open again. This time it wasn't her grandmother's face before her. Not the face of the Marguerite Delacroix that she knew, anyway.

Sensations rippled over her body and Roz knew with absolute certainty the feelings were not her own. Vignettes from a life other than hers flashed before her eyes.

A young, dark-haired woman recoiled when people tried to shake her hand or touch her.

An older gray-haired woman slid a ring onto the younger dark-haired girl's finger, then pinned a brooch to her shirt. Held her face and kissed each eye, and then her lips.

People smiling as she walked through the streets of the Quarter. She waved and even shook hands with minimum pain.

Being kissed while wearing a white-lace wedding dress.

Screams during childbirth.

Tears over an open grave surrounded by three adult children.

A five-year-old Roz smiled and wrapped her small arms around her. Around Flora. Those were all snippets of her grandmother's life. How was that even possible?

Their mouths unlocked with a pop, and steam rose from both of their lips.

The sheer force snapped Gran's body backward, and Roz landed on the floor with the realization her grandmother had once been like her … unable to touch or be touched.

Flora pushed herself up on shaky arms, waving away the faint wisps of smoke. "Remember these words, Justice. You are the Judge and the Jury. Let judgment be swift and let it be fair."

Rubbing her face, Roz stayed on the floor, then tentatively touched her tongue with her forefinger. It felt three sizes too big and a little tender. Nothing some ice couldn't handle.

Fauna squatted down next to her and rubbed her shoulder. "You okay?"

Roz nodded.

With a last pat, Fauna said, "I'll get you some water."

"With ice, please." Each word was said with a lisp. It sounded more like, *"Wih thice, lezz."*

Just great.

"It's done, now. Just sit. Arness, come." Fauna patted her leg to call the cat when she reached the open door.

Clover took two steps back. The cat growled as she paced in front of Clover, and on the last pass, whipped her tail, striking the woman's calf. If Roz's mother hadn't been wearing those jeans, the hit looked like it would have left a welt. Who knew? It might still, judging by the way her mother grimaced. Once her great aunt and the hellcat were through the door, her mother rushed to the bed.

It was a moment on the cusp of cataclysmic proportions.

Roz and Clover barely got along under the best of circumstances, and that would be them not talking at all. Before she could get out of the way, Clover's cowboy boot heel connected with her thigh.

Roz screamed in pain and clutched her leg as she shrieked, "Mom!"

It would be nice if she could say this behavior wasn't normal from her mother, but it was. Her leg didn't feel broken, but it hurt. Clover didn't look back as she berated Roz.

"You shut up! I can't believe you came here without telling me. And you," she lorded over an obvious worn-out Flora, "Mother, why? It should've been me."

"Daughter, it was never you," Flora said with an audible exhale.

Exhaustion was written all over Gran's face. However, Roz couldn't tell if it was from the ritual or this conversation. It seemed Gran and her mother had had this conversation more than once.

"It certainly shouldn't be her." Clover gestured towards Roz. "Mother, I did everything. *Everything*, so that you'd pick me. I even opened a dumb flower shop when I moved away, to prove my dedication."

Roz stood on shaky legs. "But you never worked at the shop. I did."

"Shut up, Rozlyn."

Gran shook her head with a wan smile, then closed her eyes. "Clover, it's done. Go home. I'm tired."

Roz couldn't believe her eyes as Clover grabbed her mother by the arms and shook her.

Shook her.

It was one thing to hit her, but no one should ever lay a hand on their elders and most certainly not her grandmother.

Without thought or apparent care for her safety, Roz pulled at her mother's arm, but only managed to latch onto the woman's sweater sleeve.

Which was a mistake.

Clover wasn't a small woman in height or weight, and she went to the gym every day. When her hand connected with Roz's cheek, her teeth might have rattled. Her mother had always been strong, but the backhand lifted her off the floor and tossed her against the dresser.

It was amazing she could move at all after the ritual her Gran performed, but after that lick, Roz was going to have to stay put for a minute. Her muscles rippled like water, and she was sure her bones had melted away. There was no way she could ever stop her mother, not when she was in a frenzy. If ever she could be strong, now was the time.

A growl was the only warning Clover got. Arness moved faster than a Porsche, going zero to sixty in four steps.

"Shit." Glasses crashed on the hardwood floor as Fauna followed suit. "No bite, Arness! We talked about this."

The lamp was in pieces, but the nightstand broke Clover's fall as she scuttled to back away from the pissed-off cat. To the ocelot's credit, she didn't bite, but there was an ongoing cacophony of growls. Arness held her claws over Clover's throat. It didn't matter how strong her mother was, one knick from those sharp claws and she would bleed out in an instant.

"Get off her." Fauna held her hands out, then circled around the cat. Pressing her face closer to her prey, Arness hissed again and whipped her tail with a snap. "We agreed when you came to live here that you wouldn't hurt family. Well, horrible as this one is, she's still family."

Arness turned her head in Fauna's direction, and they stared at each other. It was fascinating, really, the way Fauna communicated with the creature.

"Clover, she wants you to apologize."

"She wants me to do what?" Clover lifted her head, but the claws were still pressed against her throat, so she stopped moving. "Why?"

"She thinks of herself as our protector, and you were hurting what she considers hers."

If Clover's eyes could roll any farther back in her head, they might have. "Fine. I'm sorry."

Arness whipped her tail one last time before moving to stand next to Fauna. Clover flipped her hair, ran her hand through it to fix it, then smoothed her blouse one sleeve at a time, like nothing had happened.

Roz pulled herself up and looked at all the women in the room. Then she focused her eyes on her mother. "If you want it that badly, we can do the ritual, or whatever that was, again. I'll give it to you."

The crease in Clover's brow deepened, her lip curled, and her eyes seemed to fill with hate as she glared. "You're useless."

Roz had been on the backside of her mother's hand many times, but didn't recall ever seeing such animosity before. She didn't understand what was so special about this gift.

"Rose, it doesn't work like that, and your mother knows it. She's just being *dramatical*," Flora said.

Clover glared at Flora from the end of the bed. More than anything, Roz wanted her mother to leave.

Flora never took her eyes off Clover. "Now, Rose, do what you promised me."

Roz moved closer to her grandmother's side. "I can't go right now," she whispered, watching her mom with wariness. "Mom's gone crazy."

"I heard that, Rozlyn Pearl. Get the hell out of here and let the adults talk." Clover sneered.

Roz stared open-mouthed at the woman before her. Clover and she had never had the best relationship, but she'd never been so hostile. "Mom, what's wrong with you?"

"You have no idea what she's given you. None!" Clover yelled.

"Then why doesn't someone tell me?" Roz crossed her arms over her chest.

"I ain't telling you a goddamned thing. You have it now and it will destroy you. I'll be right here laughing when it does. You'll have no choice but to give it to me then but I might not be so willing to take the burden off your hands then."

"Gran?" Roz knelt down. "What is she talking about?"

"You'll be fine. I'll explain it to you later. Something your mother should've done years ago," Gran said. "I think your mother and I need to have a come-to-Jesus. Go on and get now. You don't want to miss the show."

Roz was welded to the spot. She wasn't leaving her grandmother and great aunt when her mother was acting like she'd lost her damned mind.

She'd only seen her mother act this erratic once before. On Roz's thirteenth birthday. Clover had had a throw-down, knockout fight with Gran at her birthday party. During the night, she snatched Roz out of her bed and moved the family to Houston.

"Don't even bother, old woman." Clover pointed at Roz, "And you—don't even bother coming home. You are dead to me." Clover swiped the vase of different roses from the dresser as she stormed out.

"Gran, you okay?"

"I'm fine, child. Your mother has always been a bit of a drama queen," Flora said with a sad smile. Worry was written all over her face as she stared at the empty door.

"Can you explain to me what's going on?"

"I will, but later. Between the rite and your mother," Flora paused, "It really took a lot out of me. Go listen to that band for me."

What she performed was called a *rite*. Okay, that's something she could look up later. At this point, Roz just wanted answers not to listen to music. "Gran?"

Her grandmother had laid back and closed her eyes.

Aunt Fauna touched Roz's shoulder. "You really should go. She's exhausted."

"But——"

"At the very least," Fauna cut her off, "...you should go have a drink. Heck, have one for me too, and record that band. She really does love the blues."

Resigned, Roz sighed and walked out. This was a two-margarita night, plus that drink Gran suggested. Anything to help cool her still flaming tongue and her curious mind.

3

———————————

THE THORNY ROSE

Entering The Thorny Rose was like taking a trip back in time. Roz thought she'd stepped into a 1930s speakeasy. Red and black brocade material lined the walls. The vine-wrapped wall sconces exuded a soft, buttery light and flickered as if powered by gas. As she walked farther inside, she looked around in awe, but then she saw it and tears filled her eyes at its beauty. The bar was the *pièce de résistance*. Rows of bottles of alcohol covered the entire back wall. The golden lighting and back mirror made the bottles look like a work of art. The long, dark wooden bar was lit at the floor, but she couldn't see much of anything else. There were too many legs in the way.

In her haste to leave Gran's house, she'd forgotten to grab her gloves. She had a pair she wasn't fond of in the glove compartment; black satin, which went to her elbows. Every time she put them on, she looked like she should be smoking a cigarette through an extra-long filter holder while wearing a mink stole. She looked pretentious in them, but they would do in a pinch.

By the time Roz parked the car and stood in the line that spanned down half a block, the band was already on stage.

If she'd thought getting in was hard, creating a path through to the bar without getting stepped on and jostled about made her feel like a master cartographer.

For the life of her, Roz couldn't figure out why her grandmother would send her here. It wasn't just for the music and drinks. She could have gone to any local bar in the Lower Garden District for that. Roz's foot patted along with the drumbeat as she waited to get to the bar. The band was wonderful, but more of rock with some blues and R&B tossed in for a kick ass set.

She stood behind a rambunctious lot getting tequila shots. After one deep inhale, she covered her nose. The shawl protected her from more than being touched. Even through the material, her nostrils burned from the funk. It was amazing how some people thought using soap and water should be optional.

Once the rowdy guys downed their shots and took away a pitcher of beer, three empty stools appeared. Roz slid into the middle seat and waited for the dark-haired bartender. She pulled out her cellphone and touched the screen to record the band. Her foot patted to the beat.

Roz hadn't heard this version of the old zydeco tune. *'Don't Mess With My...'* She patted her hand in the air twice, hitting an imaginary horn for the last part of the line.

About a minute into the next song, the bartender appeared. "Hey."

She jumped to stop the recording and her shawl slipped off her shoulders. "I'm sorry."

"You can't-" He broke off mid-sentence, eyes landing on her chest.

"I was just…" She fumbled with her phone and her shawl. "Just trying to—"

He cut her off. "No, no. It's okay."

"My Gran really likes this band," Roz offered for no reason.

It took a minute for her to get herself together. When she finally looked at the bartender, he was staring at her brooch. She took the opportunity to look at the man. He had an overall scruffy look to him: five o'clock shadow, wild dark hair, hazel eyes, not too tall, but broad through the shoulders. He seemed paralyzed for an uncomfortable ten count.

Roz fingered the trinket. "Um, it was my grandmother's."

That seemed to snap him out of it. He blinked and his eyes flickered from hazel to a luminous green. It reminded her of a wild animal.

Was that a trick of the light? How did he do that?

A woman called from farther down the bar, "Hey, can I get a whiskey sour?"

Scruffy Bartender seemed to jump to fix the other woman's drink. When he returned, he seemed to have gotten himself together. There was a half attempt at a smile, which came off wolfish and sort of unnerved Roz. "What can I get … I'm sorry. I just can't believe you're here."

Roz looked around to confirm whom he was addressing, although the man was looking directly at her when he spoke.

He grabbed a white kitchen towel from under the back bar, then wiped his hands. Never taking his gaze from hers, he walked towards her. Without warning, he touched her gloved hand. Instinct had her snatching it out of his grasp.

"Hey!" Roz rubbed the spot where he'd touched her. There wasn't any pain.

Thank goodness she had on her gloves, but a slight throb was beginning in the back of her head. Learning some truths about her family, becoming whatever *this* was. It was all too much. This entire day had been stressful. Maybe being touched was the straw.

Before she could say more, a well-dressed blond man walked behind the bar and stood with his back towards her as he talked to the bartender. There was something about this place. Everyone was extremely good looking — supernaturally so — and most gave off a vibe she couldn't put her finger on. Roz smiled at the man bun tied at the back of his head. If a man had their hair in a tight chignon like that, she pictured him as a surfer dude or carrying a *murse* (man purse). This guy didn't give her that vibe at all. Tilting her head, she admired his physique as his broad shoulders flexed in a tailored vest.

She shook her head. What was wrong with her? Never had she ogled a man, and she hadn't even seen his face. What kind of trouble would she be in then?

After getting two pats on the shoulder, Scruffy Bartender stepped out from behind the taller man, looked at her with sad eyes, and gave her a slight bow before walking away.

Goodness, did my outburst get him in trouble?

She hoped not and had every intention of telling the well-dressed man that. "Excuse me."

"*Oui, mademoiselle.*"

French? He spoke real French. That didn't sound like Cajun.

Don't get your knickers in a bunch. He probably only knows three phrases and with those words, every woman here would drop her panties.

Nope, she wasn't falling for it. But that didn't stop her from wanting to see this French Casanova.

Behind her, Roz heard the telltale sound of someone heaving. It was too late by the time she turned around.

Trapped by the bar, Roz cringed as warm puke hit her shoulder and ran down her arm. She almost threw up when specks of vomit splatter hit her cheek, even though her face had been turned away. There were no words.

"*He-he*. Oops." The girl covered her mouth with her hand, and must have smelled something foul, because she began to heave again.

Roz slipped in vomit as she got out of the way of the next projectile. "Oh, no."

If she could've detached her arm, she would have, but instead held it extended as far from herself as she could, holding the shawl with two fingers. She jumped off the stool and the dense crowd that was wall-to-wall packed moments ago, parted as if she were Moses and her shawl the staff.

"Get her out of here!" French Casanova yelled from behind her.

Roz could listen to him all night … any *other* night. All she wanted to do now was get the alcohol pungent puke off her. Of course, the line of women objected when she walked past them into the restroom, but all of that noise ceased when she held the shawl out. Hands whipped up to cover their noses in a hurry and complaints stopped. Her shawl was powerful, shutting down cranky women at first whiff. Funky, but powerful.

After taking a bath and doing her laundry in the sink, she trashed the satin gloves. Roz was ready to call it a night. Her cardigan was a lost cause, too. She wanted to burn the entire outfit. This could not have been what her grandmother had in mind when she sent her out on this adventure.

With a fistful of paper towels, Roz continued to wipe her shirt as she walked out of the restroom … and almost collided with a burly, bear of a man. He looked like a bodyguard, or maybe the bouncer, judging by his black slacks and black button down. "Oh. I'm sorry."

When she tried to go around him, the man bowed.

"Miss, the owner saw what happened to you and wanted to apologize. He'll pay for getting those items cleaned," he directed towards the cardigan and shawl on her arm, "or buying you something new. Your choice."

Roz waved him off with a smile. "No, no, that's unnecessary."

"Please. It would upset my boss if you didn't at least get your drink." He held his hand out towards an empty side cocktail table.

Roz could see the man was trying to do his job, and in truth she wanted to try the drink Gran went on about. "Dammit it," she mumbled. "I can't remember what Gran told me to order."

He laughed at her consternation, but she could tell it wasn't with malice. "I think they have that covered. Mama Flora always gets the same drink," the big man said.

"You know my gran?"

He pulled out the tall chair, and she hopped up on it. "Everyone knows her."

Drinking, rock-blues music, hanging out in a bar enough so everyone knew her name … Roz was going to have a serious talk with *Mama Flora*. The woman had another life she knew nothing about.

"Sorry about the troubles. Have a goodnight." He bent in a slight bow.

What's with all the bowing? Maybe that's something they do here.

She had been away from New Orleans for a while.

Before he walked away, he gave her a brief smile and two long canines slid past his bottom lip. Roz blinked, then blinked again, her mind racing. Were those fangs? Is this what Gran meant about this not being the world she knew?

Scruffy Bartender chose that moment to appear, carrying a small tray with a lavender glass shaker, a martini glass, and a few other accoutrements. She watched him closer now, yet nothing else seemed strange about him. He did have an energy about him which brushed against her skin, but that was true of most of the people in this bar.

After setting down the tray, Scruffy placed a rose shaped coaster in front of her with a double-sized, chilled martini glass atop it. He grabbed a metal shaker, giving it a couple of shakes before tossing it up. The glass container flipped around in the air twice before he shifted and caught it behind his back.

The watching crowd went crazy, almost screaming louder for the bartender than for the band. With a quick twist, he removed the top and a faint pink concoction poured into the glass. He was fast, faster than the average Joe Schmoe, but that's when she saw it. His eyes flickered to a bright amber and his hands blurred from speed. On her face, she could feel a slight breeze on her face as if a fan was on blowing on low. Roz didn't know what he was exactly, but dollars to beignets, he wasn't all the way human.

Odd that the idea of this place being full of supernatural creatures didn't scare her. Maybe because her own family was a little weird, too.

A girl screamed, "I want whatever she's having!"

Roz reached for the drink, but Scruffy thrust his hand out to stop her.

"Not yet," he said.

From the small dish, he picked up a red, sugared gumdrop, cut it, then wedged half of it on the rim like a lemon. He opened a small bottle and filled the empty shot glass next to his work of art with a golden liquid. He waved his hand at the drinks with a flamboyant, "Voilá."

Now that it was ready, she wanted to drink it, but hesitated. "What is it?"

"A Dewberry Gumdrop martini with a tequila chaser, but we call it, The Confessor. On the house, of course." He lowered his head and bowed, before saying, "Sorry about earlier. I'm new and here and I'd never met the Justice before." He bowed one more time before leaving her.

Justice.

It was a word her grandmother used during the *rite.*

"Do this Justice." When she'd heard it, Roz thought Gran meant to be fair to people in general, not this.

A hundred different thoughts went through her head as it all sank in. She took a long sip of the cool concoction, then another to finish it.

She was the Judge and Jury.

4

THE THIEF

The Confessor cocktail soothed Roz's tongue better than any ice cube. It worked like magic. The pain vanished by the time she finished the drink.

Good call, Gran.

Without her gloves and shawl, she felt kind of naked, plus that light buzzing persisted in the back of her mind. She'd grabbed her things to go when a wave of energy rolled over her entire body. The force of it made her stagger when she got off the chair.

What the hell was that?

It felt like ants crawling under her skin, but Gran would have said someone had just walked over her grave. Roz scanned the room and found the source of her discomfort. She eased back onto her seat and watched.

A guy about five-ten with dark brown hair and a brown leather bomber jacket moved through the crowd. Nothing about him screamed *I'm stomping on your grave,* but she knew it was him. More astute about his every move now, she observed as he winked at the girls near him, flirted, downed shots with *new* friends, and then picked their pockets.

A thief.

A young lady in all red delivered a fresh drink to Roz.

"Tell the bartender thank you. I'm leaving after this one." She slipped a ten onto the girl's tray and smiled.

Roz smirked over her drink as she watched the thief work the people near her. She slid off her seat when he moved farther away from her. He kept robbing folks throughout the bar. This wouldn't end well. She didn't have to be a psychic to see that coming. No one suspected a thing yet, but his luck would run out soon. Preparing for trouble, she placed her unfinished drink on the bar.

The ants along her skin went into overdrive. She had a gnawing obsession to do something she had never wanted to do before. Without hesitation, Roz reached out and grabbed his wrist before his hand slipped into another open purse.

"You really should give all that back."

Roz braced for the pain that always came with touching someone, but nothing happened.

He tried to jerk his arm back as he looked around as to see if anyone had noticed them.

Still holding onto him, she found she didn't want to let him go.

"Lady, I *gots* no idea what you're talking about," he whispered in an angry New York accent, as he tried to snatch his arm free again.

Surprising herself, her grip tightened. A warmth began where she held him and knowledge of him flowed into her, much like what had happened with Gran.

Vignettes of his life flickered in her mind. A young dark-haired boy walking hand in hand with an older man in Times Square. The man bumps into someone, apologizes, then pulls back, showing the young boy a wallet. No mother in the few pictures around the filthy one-room apartment. Sorrow filled the boy anytime he thought about her. As a teen, a drunk father slapped him, but he refuses to leave the man, he's all that the young man has in this world. Both were in tattered clothes, homeless, and living on the streets. Him today, searching for his father. Dread consumes him every time someone mentions visiting New Orleans.

He jerked away, yanking her out of the vision. Being pulled out with such abruptness made Roz feel like she was falling from a ten-story building. Bracing for impact, she grabbed the edge of the bar. If she hadn't, she and the floor would have gotten up close and personal.

The thief rubbed his wrist. "What did you do to me?"

What the hell is he?

"Me?" Roz mumbled. She didn't know what he was talking about. Just like the ants under her skin, she had the feeling that she needed to help him. Maybe she needed to get him to give back what he stole. Maybe that's why she felt honor-bound towards him.

He moved to get past her, and she reached out. Holding up his hands, he stopped. "Don't touch me!"

Those three words hurt her, and she couldn't understand why. It didn't matter. She had a mission, and she would complete it. Maybe then this tingling throughout her body would stop.

She followed behind him. "Then you really should return the wallets you took."

"If it gets you off my back, fine. I'll turn them into lost and found." He moved towards the exit.

Of course, he didn't slow down at the lost-and-found desk. She tapped his shoulder, and he froze. He tried to ditch her in the crowd and nearly succeeded.

"Forget something?"

She heard him mumble, then let out a string of curses, but

sure enough, he turned around and unloaded his haul. The girl in the booth's eyes widened as he pulled wallets from different pockets throughout his jacket. The man had no qualms about bumping and pushing people as he stormed outside.

30

5

INTO THE QUARTER

What am I doing? Roz thought as she followed the thief out of The Thorny Rose.

Roz couldn't believe she'd touched a complete stranger, and even worse, that she wanted to do it again. She wanted to so much, in fact, she felt like a bit of stalker as she dipped in and out through the crowd, keeping an eye on him.

At last, her long legs were finally good for something, like catching up to him. He didn't slow down, nor did he look her way.

He glared straight ahead as he seethed. "Why are you following me?"

Roz had asked herself this a few times tonight, but still didn't have a good answer. She went with the first thing that came to her. "That was a good thing you did back there."

On a primal level, she felt like this man needed her, but she would not tell him that. Her world had been askew ever since Gran told her about her family and gave her this *gift*.

"And I find you interesting," she added.

He halted.

Did I say too much?

At first, he looked like he was about to cuss her out, but upon taking a second look, she thought maybe he was he having a panic attack. His eyes went wide, shifting from side to side.

"Shit."

Before Roz could look around to see what had freaked him out, he slammed her against the wall and locked lips with hers. His lips knew French, Italian, and every romance language in between. Her condition made it impossible to touch anyone, let alone kiss them. But here she was, kissing a stranger and not feeling any pain. Even though she'd never been kissed before, she'd seen enough romance movies and read enough romance novels to know when a man had a master's degree in smooching. He tasted sweet and hot, warming her inside and out.

After what seemed like five minutes in paradise, he snatched away from her, halting the kiss with such abruptness to look scan the area. She didn't know this man but being without his touch left her feeling cold. His body unclenched and he released a small exhale, peppermint schnapps filling the air between them.

She stayed quiet as she took in his profile. Clean shaven, one deep dimple in his chin, and his lower lip was a little fuller than his top. The thing she liked the most was his hair. One side was shaved, and the side part allowed the longer hair to cover the left side of his face. Her fingers tingled to be the person to move that hair and look into those gray eyes.

He pulled away from the wall and stared at Roz. Giving her the once over from head to toe, he shivered. "What did you just do to me?" His words were breathy as his finger stroked her bottom lip.

She sucked in a breath as she shook her head. "Nothing."

Her words came out as breathy as his, but that felt like a lie on her tongue. She was on fire for this man, and hoped he felt just as out of control.

"Oh, you did something." He stroked her lip again. "All I want to do now is kiss you."

"Then do it."

Before she got the last word out, his mouth was on hers again. As good as the first kiss was, it still didn't compare to what the second held. This kiss was making her promises, and she wanted him to keep every last one.

Someone yelled, "Get a room!"

The intensity of it all scared her. Of course, at this rate, they *would* need a room.

Both were breathing hard after they pulled apart from a kiss which should have meant nothing. Except Roz felt like it was the beginning of everything.

He sighed, but still hadn't pulled away. "You might be a reason to stay in this fucked up city, but I have business here, then I'm out."

Her gaze followed his lips. When she finally looked into his eyes, he winked, then walked away.

Still against the wall, Roz didn't follow him this time. The kiss was unexpected and glorious, but also, he didn't need her anymore. Was this how her new power worked? Feelings? Premonitions? Helping people? Her grandmother said it was a gift, but right now, it felt more like a curse. She was so confused.

Blending into the crowd, the thief had only taken a few steps away from her when two large black SUV's brakes screeched. He turned to run the other direction, but a dark-skinned, bald man in black jeans and a black tee stopped in front of her, blocking his way.

Roz didn't dare move.

The passenger door of the first SUV opened and a man in a blue suit got out. "Well, well, Saint Montenegro. You're not the man I was looking for, but you'll do." He strolled over to the second SUV and banged on the passenger door.

A tall, lean man with a green mohawk, dressed in all black got out.

The man in blue, hands in his pockets, walked back to the first SUV and leaned against the door.

Saint held his hands up. "Nicolas … Nick … bud, you don't have to do this, you know. I was going to bring back the money."

"I think we're a little," Nick held his thumb and forefinger close together but not quite touching, "… past that point now. Come on, the boss would love to talk to you."

"I'm kind of busy."

"We saw." Nicolas snapped his fingers and pointed in Roz's direction, then yelled, "Calvin!" He turned around and got back into the first SUV.

That guy pointed at her. What does that mean?

Calvin, the pasty white man with the green mohawk, grinned as he unsnapped a slender metal baton from his belt. "With pleasure."

He flicked his wrist, and the small stick went from about eight inches and expanded to about two feet long, if not longer. Saint didn't have a chance. Calvin swung wide and hit him with wild abandon across the head multiple times, lashed his torso, then the side of his knees. Saint crumbled to the ground and Calvin dragged him by the arm towards the waiting vehicle, where he threw him in.

Roz looked around with wild eyes as the green-haired guy assaulted Saint and abducted him. *Was she next?* She opened her mouth to scream, but the big, dark-skinned man in all black nearest her grabbed her arm.

"You going too, sista," the big man drawled. "Don't fight me. We ain't got time for that."

Roz gulped as enormous arms wrapped around her. Despite what he'd said, she still struggled against his tight grip. If she fought too much, she sensed he could break her arm. A coolness emanated from where he held her arm behind her back.

Images moved through her mind like a flip book, stopping at different stages in his life. *His name is Lester. He grew twice as fast as others his age, but for years he took his favorite toy, a stuffed polar bear, everywhere. It was gift from his father who disappeared mysteriously. Mom worked multiple jobs, but one was always as a waitress. She kissed his cheek before walking away. Lester as a teen, being slapped around by Mom's boyfriend. Mom's mascara runs from tears getting between her man and her son, asking Lester to forgive him. Someone performed a rite over him.*

Roz didn't know what Lester was, but she was sure he didn't know either.

Lester's eyes widened as he stared down at her. "What was that?" He closed his eyes, exhaled, then released her arm. After a full body shake, he opened his eyes. "I'm so sorry about this," he whispered. "Nick would have my head if I let you go."

Something in Roz compelled her to touch his cheek. There wasn't pain so much as a tingling sensation, much like static electricity thrumming any place her skin connected to his. She knew he was telling the truth. Lester leaned into her touch the way she always did with Gran. It had been a long time since anyone showed this man any affection. He looked like a big, ferocious bear, but he had a gentle heart.

"I won't let anything happen to you. Just come with us."

Lester took her arm, less rough, as he led her to the SUV's opening.

The big man extended his hand to help her, but she reached in and crawled into the seat of her own accord. This might be a huge mistake, but Roz sat down next to the man who still needed her. The SUV door needed WD-40 or some type of lube because the screech reminded her of a prison cell door slamming behind them.

6

FIRST DATE FOR THE AGES

R oz was bound, gagged, and covered in a black canvas bag. She inhaled the potent scent of cannabis with every breath. Which could be the reason she was calm in this crazy situation. Once inside the SUV, Calvin had tied old rags in their mouths and slapped the bags over their heads.

The driver seemed to hit every bump in the road, tossing her into her co-hostage for most of the ride. She felt tendrils of ice when she touched Lester, but flicks of flame licked at her soul when she came near Saint. What made him different when they touched? She extended her fingers, grazing Saint's before he snatched his hand away. The ride seemed a little longer after that.

Calvin shook his head. "I thought we were supposed to be off tonight. What the hell is up with Nick?"

"That's right, you missed the shit-show. He vouched for someone who screwed the boss. Nicky is in C-Y-A mode."

The driver had a slow, high-pitched drawl that was the total opposite of Calvin's raspy tenor. Roz could tell exactly who was speaking. However, she didn't detect any supernatural energy like Lester's. These two men were scary, but still just human.

Calvin growled out. "*Fils putain!*"

Son of a bitch was right, Roz thought as she sat listening. *What the hell is Saint mixed up in?*

After seeing Lester's life, Roz knew they were in trouble. If they blinked wrong at his boss, the man would kill them. Listening seemed like the best tool she could utilize to ensure her survival.

"Yeah, that *couyon* stole the shipment, the money, and tried to strike a new deal with the supplier."

The driver seemed all too happy to talk.

Lester groaned behind her. Didn't sound like he was a fan of what they were discussing.

"Is that why I've been working at the bait house this last month?"

"I 'ont know."

"He dead?"

The driver groaned out an, "Un-un."

Lester cleared his throat. "There are ears here."

"It doesn't matter what they hear," Calvin said. "The boss is in a mood and it ain't a good one."

Saint stiffened next to her. At first, she didn't understand what Calvin meant, but it became clear they were *not* getting out of this alive.

When the SUV finally came to a stop, and the doors opened, bullfrogs and crickets were all Roz could hear. They'd left the sounds of the city and the crowds of

Mardi Gras a while back. At least, it felt that way. It was hard to decipher time and distance from under a hood.

"Bring 'em in, Les," Calvin barked.

The fresh scents of pine and cypress were faint against the potent stench of brackish water. They were near the swamp.

Is this the bait house?

Unease rolled through her not only because of where she assumed they were, but because Saint hadn't said a word since getting into the SUV.

Lester's hand touched hers, and she flinched.

"I told you I'm not going to hurt you," he whispered.

He'd mistook her reaction for fear. True, she was scared, but that wasn't why she'd recoiled. A vision now would be inconvenient, but luck was on her side for once, and nothing happened. She hoped her gift had more to it than visions. Some supernatural strength or telekinesis would be awesome right about now.

Lester removed the bags from Roz and Saint's heads, but only removed her plastic zip-ties and gag, leaving Saint's in place.

Roz rubbed her wrists to get some circulation going to her numb hands. After being in total darkness for so long, it took a few minutes for her eyes to focus. She squinted while Lester led them to a small building. They were deep in the woods, surrounded by the dark shaped cypress and tall pine trees. The only light came from the headlights shining on the small, windowless structure.

Dry grass, pines needles, and small rocks crunched under their feet as they made their way to the door. It had crossed Roz's mind more than once to run, but run where? She looked at the dark, dense woods on three sides of her and then at the homemade dock dead-ending into a swamp.

Gator country.

Nope. She had to think of another way out and maybe once they were alone, Saint would snap out of this funk and help her.

Lester stood to the side of the door, tore the rag from Saint's mouth and cut his binds with a pocket knife. He halted Roz with an outstretched hand. "I know what you heard, but I'm going to do everything in my power to get you out alive. I promise."

Roz gave him a sad smile, because she knew he was being honest and would try to help her. "I know."

I just hoped it will be enough.

The door slammed shut behind them and the small room fell into darkness. A loud series of *clanks* and *clicks* from the various locks resounded through the silent room.

Roz felt along the wall as Saint rattled the door. Banging on it with his hand, he yelled, "Son of a bitch!"

Well, she was glad he was back online. The room was about the size of a small bedroom, sans windows. There were no tools, but she was surprised when her fingers touched a concrete floor, then fumbled over a metal grate or drain. She snatched her fingers back. There was something wet and sticky in the grate.

"Ugh, that's so gross." A million thoughts of what it could be flowed through her mind, but only one seemed to be the correct answer.

Blood.

Exploring in a place that she couldn't even see her hands in front of her face was no good. She might find something worse than blood. She patted her way back to the wall, stating, "We got to get the fuck out of here." Then, adding, "What did you steal from them?" She waited. It took so long, she didn't think he would answer.

A whoosh of air moved over her. He was pacing in front of her.

"No." The answer came clipped, but she heard more than that one word.

"Come. Sit."

She extended her hand, although he couldn't see it, but he bumped into her and stopped. It seemed like forever, but it finally took it and sat down next to her. Even after sitting, he didn't let her hand go. A warm energy pulsated from where they were connected. The heat between them brought her a certain type of peace.

"Whatever it is, you can tell me."

Saint brought her hand to her to his cheek. "Your hand is so warm."

There was nothing she could say. If she stayed quiet, maybe he would tell her what kind of mess they were tangled up in.

"What are you doing to me?"

She didn't answer. Mostly because she didn't know how to answer, so she lifted her shoulder in a small shrug. Saint's fingers rubbed over her knuckles in a rhythm. She wasn't sure if he'd even noticed his actions.

"You make me want to tell you everything," he whispered.

Both of Roz's brows lifted. A desire to confess all that must be part of the gift as well. "My Gran's a good listener. I'm sure I get it from her."

"This is all my dad's fault. He called me, told me he had a big score and to come join him. That was three months ago. What they were talking about? Yeah … I'm sure that's why I'm here. They want whatever he stole from them."

She dreaded to think what type of condition his father was in. "Sounds like he's still alive, though. That's good, right?"

A painful laugh bubbled out of him. "Yeah, sure, but for how long?"

"Don't think like that. We're going to get out of this. I'm sure if they wanted you dead, you would be already."

Using both hands, Roz turned his head towards hers. Although they couldn't see each other, the warmth of his breath was enough to keep her going. He was listening. She was sure of it.

"They brought us here to intimidate us. Scare us. I must admit they've done a bang-up job of that, but when they ask you for whatever it is they want, that'll be our opportunity to get away."

God, I hope so.

His fear tightened around her heart like a vice and all she wanted to do was soothe him. "You really think so?"

"Absolutely."

Before she could stop herself, she leaned in and pressed her lips to his. Even in the dark, she reached his lips, and not his nose, on the first try. She was getting better at this kissing thing.

Or not.

Roz closed her eyes and grabbed her head after it dipped. It could have been low blood sugar, an oncoming headache, or even rag-weed allergies, but when a voice spoke in her mind, she knew it was something different.

It was her damned gift.

The urge to speak the words out loud burned in her. Words old as time and more powerful than anything she could comprehend.

Ritual words.

As the words came to her, now she understood. The words were meant for the man who could complete her. She closed her eyes and let her forehead touch his.

Saint pulled away. "What's that? Latin?"

Roz slapped her hands over her mouth as a bright light lit them up.

"Aw, look at the lovebirds. Come on, you two," Calvin jeered. "Time to die."

7

PLAN B, C, & D

One thing Roz hated with a passion—bullies. Right now, Calvin was the biggest bully in the room. If they got out of this alive, Roz was going to visit his ass with Arness.

They weren't in the SUV long, but they did, however, get the black bag treatment again. The crickets and frogs were having a swamp concerto. Once out of the vehicle, it took a moment for to get solid footing as the gravel pebbles moved under her shoes. The screeching sound of metal grinding on metal made Roz's ears bleed. Even out in the swamp, they could've put some grease on those tracks to stop that infernal noise.

With a shove, Roz bumped into Saint as they were pushed inside, and the bags snatched from their heads. Pulling some of her hair in the process, Calvin smiled with a perverse pleasure. She was positive he knew exactly what he'd done.

After a few blinks, her eyes focused on where they were. Calvin and Lester were behind them and Nick, in a fresh, red, three-piece-suit, was in front of them. She looked beyond him to see inside. It was an old airplane hangar they seemed to be using as a storage facility.

With his hands in his pockets, Nick turned to them, but stood in front of Saint. "Mr. Renoir would like to speak to you. Don't speak unless spoken to or she will be shot. Flinch like you want to attack our boss and she will be shot, and then you will be shot. Do you understand?"

Saint rolled his eyes but gave a curt nod.

The *clicks* of Calvin's expandable baton resonated in the air behind Roz. She turned to look just as he pushed Saint with the sharp arrow end.

Calvin stabbed her in the center of her back. "Keep your eyes forward."

Roz grimaced but refused to let the green-haired freak see her cry. Men with machine guns paced along the scaffolding on both sides. Underneath were rows of opened and unopened wooden containers and large plastic shipping crates. The place looked filled from end to end.

The pathways between the boxes created a maze. Nick led them around in a circle before they reached a wide, round opening in the middle of the building. Roz couldn't believe what she was seeing, but it was there all the same.

A golden king's throne chair with red velvet and a foot-stool.

A foot-stool? Really?

A man in a soot-gray, three-piece-suit sat with his legs crossed, holding a delicate teacup in his hand. An *Alfred,* the butler type in an all-black suit, poured tea from an antique stone dragon teapot.

Mr. Renoir.

The boss blew over the steaming drink, then set it on a marble side table. "Please, have a seat."

When Saint and Roz didn't move, Calvin pushed Saint, but when the pointy end of the metal baton moved towards Roz, she turned and grabbed it. "I've had enough of you and your poking stick."

"I have yet to give you a good working over with my poking stick."

She pushed the baton back at him. "You just keep your hands and stick to yourself."

"Oh, the *minou* has claws," Calvin jeered. "… and I thought you were just in heat. I like feisty cats."

Ugh. This man makes me want to murder him.

"You have a brain?"

Calvin lifted his hand, poised to backhand her. Roz didn't cringe, but just behind him she could see Lester's hand moving slowly towards his gun. With an imperceptible shake of her head, she stopped him. They weren't dying this way.

"Enough, Mr. Milton. As of right now, she's a guest," Renoir said with a pleasant smile.

Roz got the distinct impression that if this man didn't like their answers, they wouldn't be guests for too long.

Fire raged in Calvin's eyes, but he lowered his hand. "Yes, sir."

Instead, he extended one hand like an usher, but Roz side stepped his other hand when he placed it behind her. The mere thought of that man touching her made her wish she could shoot fire from her fingertips. She took a seat in the folding chair with the green-haired monster still at her side.

Calvin leaned down and whispered into her ear, "Later, *putain.*"

Renoir sipped his tea then, placed it delicately on the table. "Saint … may I call you Saint?"

The man spoke with a refined accent. No one would guess

he was from New Orleans by the way he sounded now, but little inflictions still gave him away.

"Let me get down to the point. My name is Phillippe Renoir. I run this town. Your father took something from me, and I want it back."

"Mr. Renoir, sir, I don't know what you're talking about."

Renoir finished the cup of tea and unfurled his legs. "I see. So, when your father was robbing me and plotting to take my place in New Orleans, you knew nothing about it?"

Saint took a breath to speak, but the man held up his hand, halting any response he might have had. "Be mindful of your next words. I would hate to end our association here."

Roz looked between the two men. She understood little about what was going on, but she had a fair idea what *'end our association here'* meant.

"Yes, yes, I knew something was going on," Saint stammered. "But nothing about stealing from you."

Renoir leaned back, propped his elbows on the arm of the chair, and steepled his fingers. "I'm going to give you one chance to make this right, one chance to see your father, and one chance *not* to get your young lady killed."

Roz had been listening for some opportunity to get out of this, but it only seemed to be going from bad to worse.

Saint's head turned towards her, then back to the boss. "She has nothing to do with this. I just met her."

"Lies!" Calvin blurted out from behind them. "They haven't been able to keep their hands off each other."

Drenched in anger and embarrassment, Roz jumped up. "It's nothing like that." She turned, giving Calvin the evil eye, before turning back. Her feet took small steps towards the boss all on their own. "True, I was kissing him. But I only met him tonight when he was stealing."

Renoir lifted a brow.

"Wait, I made him give the wallets back. Whatever … it doesn't matter." Her nerves were making her ramble. "What does matter … life. There's no need to kill me or him."

Renoir shook his head. "It's a shame you got caught up with this young man. Because his fate is, unfortunately, now yours."

This couldn't be happening. The truth of his words burned through her, and it made her angry. Unlike when she *wanted t*o touch Saint, this time she had the overwhelming urge to touch *him*. Mr. Renoir was going to kill them. She understood that with a glaring clarity, but it didn't stop what needed to happen right now. In three steps, she lunged for Mr. Renoir. It would be impossible to win in a fight with Nick or Calvin, but she only needed to touch him. She needed him to confess.

This would be Justice.

A voice inside her urged, no, *demanded* she judge Phillippe Renoir.

To mark him.

Another new trick with her gift. When she reached out to touch him, he backhanded her. It bloomed from her cheek, then throughout her entire body. Instead of cradling her cheek like she wanted to, she grabbed his wrist. He tried to shake her loose, but she held on for dear life.

Gunfire and chaos erupted around her.

Words like "shoot her," "get her off of him," and "don't touch her" were being yelled all around her, but she couldn't stop. Nick was running towards them, and then grabbed his butt cheek as he crumpled to the floor at the base of the throne.

There was no time to think about everything going on around her as energy pulsed from where their hands connected. Renoir stared into her eyes with horror as his life flickered through Roz's mind and through his, she suspected. A coldness flushed her body as she witnessed every murder, every theft, and every woman he'd paid, abused, and seduced.

Roz felt like a slick oil was being poured over her body as she watched his life. It was far dirtier and slimier than she could have imagined. Far worse than anything Lester or Saint had ever done. This man was human and a complete monster. A compulsion boiled up inside of her, along with revulsion. Holding herself together enough not to throw up in her mouth, she leaned in and kissed Renoir on the forehead before being snatched away.

Calvin slammed her on the floor next to a bloody Saint. Calvin held a gun and waved it between the two of them. "Boss, you okay?"

Renoir spoke like he was coming out of a drunken stupor. "What did you just do?" He wiped his forehead, then massaged his temples.

Calvin snatched her up by one arm, turning the gun towards Saint, who kept twitching.

Roz wasn't sure what she had done to him, but she had her suspicions. Still, she knew better than to speak it aloud. To speak it into existence. How could she say she marked a man for death?

"I'm not sure."

"Roz, what did you do? I feel weird." Saint stared at his hands. A green glow emanated from them. "I want to kill him. Need to finish what you started …"

Saint held his hand over the barrel of Calvin's gun, and with a bright green flare, it melted.

"What the fuck?" Calvin dropped the gun and crossed himself with the sign of the cross, but didn't let go of her.

"Oh, shit," Roz whispered. She'd done this to him. "Fight

it, Saint." She struggled in Calvin's grasp, but he held her firm. "Dammit, let me go."

"Stop squirming. You're mine."

Roz stared between Saint and the man on the throne. "Mr. Renoir, you have to let us go. I don't know what's happening, but I think his compulsion is aimed towards you."

"Kill them," Renoir yelled. "And start with that bitch."

"I've been waiting on this all night, *minou*." Calvin's hand tightened around her throat and waist. "A kitten's neck can snap so easily."

Roz was tall, but nowhere near his six-foot-five height, and he lifted her up with ease. Both of her hands scratched and pulled at the fingers, crushing her larynx. She could barely catch her breath as a bone deep coldness settled in. Genuine fear raced through her as her vision flickered in and out.

Before laying a finger on Calvin, she knew he was a killer. The connection between them felt like shards of icicles stabbing her throughout her body. They both fell to the ground. His hand was still around her throat, but with no pressure now. After taking a few deep breaths, she pried his fingers away and looked at him. His eyes bulged and his body twitched as if something had electrocuted him. Energy still moved through him.

Oh, yes. He felt the connection.

She slid her hands into his, and his life flashed before her eyes. Unlike the others, Calvin had a wonderful childhood, loving parents, middle class home, and lots of friends. Then she saw a glimpse of a younger Calvin. Even at eight he was rotten to the core, holding a kitten by the throat and squeezing.

Unable to bear what was about to happen next, Roz snatched her hand away, breaking their connection. Calvin pulled himself into a tight fetal position. She doesn't think he'd ever faced all the pain and horrible things he'd done until now. Her hand hovered above his head, but she didn't dare touch him again.

"Lester! Kill him, then grab her," Renoir demanded, pointing.

Saint struggled within Lester's arms. Mr. Renoir seemed unaware of the danger the young thief presented. Saint had murder in his eyes. Roz looked around and dived for a gun discarded in the melee, then held it out with trembling hands. Moving it from Saint and Lester to Mr. Renoir.

"All right, *cher*, no need for that," Renoir said with his hands up and a smile on his face.

"We're going to leave now." Her voice trembled as much as the gun. "Don't send anyone after us, either. Lester, you can come too. You're a good man. Come with me."

"What are you?" Renoir quipped in fascination. "A priestess, a witch? You single-handedly took out one of my best men without a weapon. You put something in my mind, and in his." He pointed to Saint.

Roz's heart tightened at whatever she'd done to Saint. Maybe because she'd only started the ritual and didn't finish that he was like this now. Her Gran would know how to fix this. She just had to get them out alive.

Roz held out her other hand. "Lester, bring him to me."

Who knew a gun could be so heavy?

Mr. Renoir watched her with wonder and something else. "I could use a girl like you. You could be my number two."

Roz couldn't believe this man.

A job offer? Really?

Saint and Lester stood beside her now. She touched his cheek, turning his head. "Saint? You doing okay?"

Saint grimaced, then nodded. The green glow in his eyes

and hands decreased once he looked away from his target, the person she'd marked.

"Give me that, baby girl." Lester took the gun out of her hand.

Thank goodness. Her hand was beginning to cramp. She slid an arm around Saint's waist. He looked as if he would collapse at any moment.

"If you would be so kind as to let Saint's dad go."

Mr. Renoir smiled as he eased back into his throne, arms spread wide. "I can't."

Saint spoke with his eyes shut tight. "What did you do to my dad?" There was a note of panic in his voice.

The man gave that *half laugh when nothing was funny* chuckle. "Oh, kid, He ain't dead. Your dad's a slippery one. He escaped last night. Nick was out looking for him when they came across you. I see family isn't as important to your father as it is to you, since you didn't know." Renoir smirked.

A faint green glow from Saint's hands started getting brighter again. "If we don't leave. I think, no, I know, I will kill him." He pulled out of Roz's grip and the pupils of his eyes went bright green as he moved past her.

Renoir seemed unfazed. "Bring it, kid."

Goodness. Roz jumped in front of Saint. She knew he would kill the man who sat smugly on his throne with his arms spread wide. Renoir had no idea what kind of trouble he was in. Saint stopped, but never looked away from his target. She slid her fingers into his hands, which were warmer than average.

"Saint? Come back to me. Saint!"

No response.

Roz didn't want to, but she slapped him. When her palm struck his cheek, he glared at her, but his eyes were a lovely shade of gray again.

"What was that for?"

"We're leaving. Now." She grabbed his now-regular-temperature hand and marched out, Lester in tow.

"You'll regret not taking my offer, *cher*." With all of his Cajun accent back, she heard Renoir yell as she walked out the door, *"You too, traitor."*

She probably would, but murder was not on the menu tonight. However, grand theft auto was. Lester rummaged through the pockets of unconscious Nick. The man groaned and moved as if he was coming to. Lester reared back and hit him. Knocking him out again.

"Nick wasn't dead? I thought you shot him," Roz said once they were on the road.

Lester chuckled. "I did … with a taser, square, dead in his ass."

Roz couldn't help but laugh. "I guess he deserved that."

"That, and then some, but my gun was empty, and he was about to reach you. Anyway, no more talk about him. Where are we going?" Lester asked with a smile on his face.

Saint touched her hand and whispered, "Can you fix me?"

"We'll see my Gran tomorrow and sort this out. Do you feel okay?"

"Sore, but supercharged."

Roz squeezed his hand. "I think you'll be fine as long as you don't see Mr. Renoir."

Roz was beyond aware she'd made a powerful enemy tonight, but gained two friends. Something in short supply in her life. Things could only go up from here.

"I don't know about you guys, but I need a drink. No, I will need at least two drinks." Roz laughed after the words were out. Her grandmother was right.

"French Quarter it is."

It was four a.m. and Mardi Gras was still in full swing.

They say Vegas is the *City that Never Sleeps*, but there's no party like a NOLA party. She needed answers and so did Saint, but they could wait until tomorrow.

For now, Confessors and tequila all around.

The End

Thank you for reading **Curses and Other Family Secrets.** I hope you enjoyed Roz's origin story. If you want to find out more about the new Justice of New Orleans. Roz's story continues in Judge, Jury, and Two Exes.

Keep reading for an exclusive excerpt of R.R. Born's
Incubus Born
&
Judge, Jury, and Two Exes
The *FIRST* Death Maiden Chronicles novel!

Still want more stories from the Death Maiden world? Grab The French Casanova bartender's origin story
Incubus Born

INCUBUS BORN EXCERPT

My body tightened from the sensations. I was close, but the climax I desired was a different sort of orgasm. I pulled my mouth away from Delilah's delectable mounds, threaded my fingers through the thick mane of pink-and-white hair bobbing in my lap, and lifted the woman off. Her mouth released me with a pop, and she groaned aloud her dissatisfaction while reaching for me again. I tightened my grip and jerked her head back to look up at me. Her lips were plump, and her pupils were blown wide open as her body hummed with sexual energy, the desire dripping off her like honey. She was ready for me.

Commanding, "Kiss me," I released her, then leaned back against the headboard.

She rose to her knees on the bed, not taking her eyes off mine, and then climbed the last few inches up my chest. I ran my hand over her petite frame, between her legs, and through her folds, coating my fingers with her wetness. The moment I touched the little bud, she screamed out.

That's when I struck.

Flipping her onto her back, my lips covered hers in a

fierce tangle of lips, teeth, and tongues. Her being wet wasn't enough, though. Her desiring me wasn't enough either. To feed the curse, I needed more. I needed a little piece of her soul. My lips greedily tugged at hers and pulled her tongue into my mouth as I sucked down her continued cries of pleasure. With every draw, her spiritual energy poured into me, melting on my tongue like warm chocolate, and she tasted just as sweet. With one last tug of her tongue, I released her.

She smiled, a goofy satisfied grin.

"No fair. Stop hogging him, Azalea," Delilah whined.

I looked over, and her bottom lip was pouted out. When I leaned her way, the woman under me moaned.

"Mmm, you're so yummy. I really want another—" Azalea's mouth opened wide as she yawned.

"I think that's enough for right now." After placing a kiss on her forehead, I crawled from on top of her.

Azalea curled up and drifted off the moment I moved. It was hard to believe the fiery sex kitten from a minute ago was now asleep like a baby.

Still pouty, Delilah offered an irresistible and tempting sight. My hands went to either side of her face, right before I sucked her plump bottom lip into my mouth. She kept moving her head from side to side, trying to deepen the kiss, but that wasn't what I wanted. With playful licks and nips, I wanted to enjoy the taste of her on my tongue, the feel of her in my mouth.

Azalea had sated the curse—I wouldn't need to feed again for a while—but there was something about this woman. Perhaps it was her long black hair. Maybe it was the way she gave herself to me without hesitation. Might have even been the way she pouted—a weakness I'd yet to outgrow in my many centuries in this world.

In an effort to take over, Delilah flung her leg over my lap and ground her sex into my groin. Then using her hands to lift my mouth to hers, her tongue tangled with mine, demanding and so unlike the gentle caresses I'd just given her. I closed my eyes and let her control the kiss while opening myself enough to allow a small bit of her essence to flow through me.

Breathless, Delilah pulled back and gazed into my eyes. "Dude, has anyone ever told you that you are like, so addictive?"

"Maybe a time or two." The tip of my tongue ran along her neck. A shiver ran through her when I sucked behind her ear, lending me more spiritual energy than I needed. My well was full.

Her hands rolled over my chest. One finger kept coming back to a sensitive spot. Not a fresh wound, but an old scar. I grabbed her fingers, sucking each into my mouth, causing her to cry out. Yet, over and over, her finger kept touching the roughened flesh, making me again move her away.

The tip of her tongue licked my neck, then she kissed the same spot. Her finger touched the spot again. "What's this?"

My eyes didn't waver or look down when I responded. "That?" I pulled Delilah's fingers away again, this time holding them. The raised skin, shaped in a horizontal infinity sign, looked as perfect as the day I'd received it. "It's a sign of my undying love."

The Thorny Rose had been the primary hub for the supernatural community in New Orleans for more than two centuries. Humans loved the place just as much as the preternaturals. They kept the place packed every weekend and twice as full during Mardi Gras. It might be the drinks or the live music, but dollars to beignets it had something to do with the unnaturally gorgeous men and women that were always in attendance.

The first time Roz came into the bar, she could hardly believe that these people were real. Now, she knew most weren't human. This was one of NOLA's best kept secrets.

Roz and Lester side-stepped the long line and walked in. Lester's broad shoulders and sheer size made people move aside as they walked to the bar. Once they got their drinks, he led her to a back corner table where she could look at the stage and the incoming flow of people. A lot of the customers looked inebriated already, but that didn't stop them from staggering straight to the bar again.

Lester found a booth and sat across from each other. He lifted his beer and Roz clinked her martini glass to his.

"Cheers."

Lester took a healthy swallow before asking, "It's just us two. You want to tell me what's really going on?"

Roz looked down, picking at the lacquer on the tabletop. It seemed to be the most interesting thing suddenly. She shook her head. "Nothing. I'm fine."

The big man hadn't made a sound. She finally looked up through squinted eyes. He frowned, leaned forward, and curled his enormous arms on the table.

Roz rushed to finish before he preached, and he would. "Okay, a few of the ladies from the community." She lifted her fingers to create air quotes for the last word. "Came to inform me that crime was on the rise and it was my fault. Apparently, some supes have been using their powers out in the open."

Lester shook his head. "What the hell?"

"I don't know what I can do about that. Les, I'm not cut out to be this Justice. One person can't police an entire city of supernatural beings. I don't want to see their deepest, darkest, vilest secrets. That shit doesn't magically go away, you know. It stays with me." She tapped her temples.

Lester rubbed his hands on his thighs. "I didn't know, but Rozlyn...your grandmother thought you could do it. She wouldn't have given you this responsibility if she thought you couldn't handle it."

Roz's sad eyes looked at his big brown ones. "I want to believe you. I want to believe Gran knew what she was doing when she gave me this power. But honestly—" She shook her head.

"While you are throwing yourself this pity party, think about this. If you hadn't touched me, I'd still be in the dark about my true nature and I'm not an evil person."

"True, but you were different. You are different," Roz interjected.

"You're right. I was worse. I was a bodyguard…among other things." Lester looked down as he garbled the last part of the sentence. "For the biggest gangster in town."

Roz couldn't say anything to that. Les had kidnapped her when she didn't even know she had powers. She accidentally unbound magic that kept his true nature a secret. Even from himself.

Lester didn't touch her, he knew from past experience no to, but waved his hand in front of her eyes to bring her back to the here and now. "Rozlyn, I can see you're scared. Hell, I know how you feel, but it doesn't stop the fact that we are who we are. No matter how much we try to hide from ourselves."

Her heart ached knowing every word he said was true. There was no way to explain that their situations were completely different. She looked him in the eyes and gave him a tight nod instead. He seemed to take that, as *it was okay*. And it pained her she couldn't tell him it really wasn't.

"Okay," he said enthusiastically.

Roz smiled, then said, "Okay."

She took a long sip from her martini. It was cool on her tongue and when the alcohol hit her system; she knew it. The tension that had held her shoulder like two taut coil springs loosened. She finished the last of the drink. They'd only known each other a few months, but Roz couldn't remember if she ever heard the big man talk this much before. Listening to him now, she felt like she was getting to know the real Lester Broussard.

A drink appeared in front of her. The chilled martini glass glowed with a blue liquid. Roz heard a growl before she looked up to the server who'd delivered the martini. She knew it was a man by the delicious cologne he wore. His scent warmed her to the very core.

"You looked thirsty, *mon amour*," a sultry deep French accent purred. "And I so hate to see a woman wanting."

Roz couldn't believe her eyes. The six foot plus, sandy-haired man was a specimen of male perfection. She wasn't sure what he was, but he was not the type to buy her a drink.

"Go away, man whore," Lester growled.

The beautiful man squinted his lavender eyes in Lester's direction. "No one's talking to you," he sniffed the air, "what is that buffalo, wildebeest?" He wrinkled his nose at Lester, then looked back at Roz. "I'm sure the new Justice can speak for herself."

This man knew what she was. *How?* Roz's hand whipped out in front of Lester to stop him from jumping across the table at the man.

Lester sat back but didn't take his eyes off the visitor. Something came over Roz. She lifted the drink, tilted it towards the visitor in a 'here's to you' salute, then turned up the martini glass like it was a shot of tequila.

"Rozlyn."

She heard Lester admonish, but she held up her other hand to ward off anymore words until she finished the drink.

Roz carefully held the empty glass out to the sexy man in front of her. His pale purple eyes seemed to deepen into amethyst as he laughed. The kind of laugh that rolled down your spine like fingers playing the scale on a piano. She squirmed in her seat, not wanting him to see what kind of affect he was having on her.

"Thank you…" Roz paused as she held his laughing eyes.

"Francois," he said, as he took the waiting glass in one hand, then slid his right hand into her gloved one.

Panic wiped away her bold facade as Roz tried to snatch

her hand away. Francois, whatever he was, was also fast. Although she wore gloves, she could feel power roll off him into her palm. She was still new to this, but his power didn't feel malicious. It felt warm and seductive.

"What are you?" Roz breathed out huskily.

A slow smile spread across Francois' face. "You *are* new if you don't know what I am."

"He's a man whore and you don't need to talk to him," Lester said while glaring at the man.

Roz tore her eyes away from Francois, but never releasing his hand. "Now, now Les. Isn't that why you brought me here? To meet new people."

"Not his kind. His kind ain't nothing but trouble," Lester said.

Finally, Roz pulled her hand from his grip, and preceded pulled off her gloves. "I need to know those as well."

"Roz, no. Anyone but him." Lester pleaded.

"It'll be okay. I have a good feeling about this," Roz said, then gave Lester a wink. "Now," she looked up at the devastatingly handsome Francois with her bare hand out. "How do you do? My name is Roz Vincent."

Instead of taking her hand, Francois went to one knee in front of her. It looked like he was ready to propose. Once he bowed his head and closed his eyes, the surrounding voices quieted. Roz only vaguely took stock of what was happening around her, because the man before her was in pain.

Without another thought, Roz's hand cradled his cheek. Her power flowed from him to her. Flashes of a life that began long before television or even electricity. Her other hand found his other cheek, and the circuit was complete. François Henri Toussaint DeChevalier was complicated, complex, harsh, and tender-hearted, and all those things would barely scrape the surface of his true nature.

A seducer of women. A sexual demon. He was literally what wet dreams were made of. François was an incubus.

So much information rushed into her, it overwhelmed all of her senses. The last thing she remembered was leaning forward to kiss his forehead, but he'd lifted his head at the same time. Their lips met, and for once, there was no pain. Roz just wanted to lounge in that feeling for a moment, but when he took control of the kiss, pulling her tongue deeper into his hot mouth. The kiss deepened and she let go of every inhibition. then her world went black.

ACKNOWLEDGMENTS

I'd like to thank the editors who helped me get this book finished - Kay Copeland and R.E. Hargrave. This book has been sitting on my laptop for the better part of five years and they helped me bring it to life. Thank you.

When I needed some last minute help, I reached out to my online writers group, League of Romance Writers and they didn't disappoint. Thank you, Wendy Cederberg, Susan Williams, Karen Burns and Ken Wallen. I appreciate you all taking time from your busy day to help me.

ABOUT THE AUTHOR

R.R. Born is the author of the highly popular, Gray Witch series. She lives in Texas with her husband, and an orange tabby terror named Pele and a rescued English Bulldog named Joey. She graduated from Houston Community College where she studied Photography, then graduated with a degree in Film and screenwriting from Long Island University in Brookville, NY. She's worked as a Production Coordinator, Second Assistant Director on local commercials, TLC & HGTV shows, and movies.

For more info on upcoming projects, sign up for my
Newsletter
www.rrborn.com